Frederick J. Furnivall

# Caxton's Book of Curtesye

SALZWASSER
VERLAG

Frederick J. Furnivall

# Caxton's Book of Curtesye

Reprint of the original.

1st Edition 2023 | ISBN: 978-3-37514-582-8

Verlag (Publisher): Salzwasser Verlag GmbH, Zeilweg 44, 60439 Frankfurt, Deutschland
Vertretungsberechtigt (Authorized to represent): E. Roepke, Zeilweg 44, 60439 Frankfurt, Deutschland
Druck (Print): Books on Demand GmbH, In de Tarpen 42, 22848 Norderstedt, Deutschland

# Caxton's Book of Curtesye.

Early English Text Society.

Extra Series. No. III.

# Caxton's
# Book of Curtesye,

PRINTED AT WESTMINSTER ABOUT 1477-8 A.D.

AND NOW REPRINTED,

WITH TWO MS. COPIES OF THE SAME TREATISE, FROM
THE ORIEL MS. 79, AND THE BALLIOL MS. 354.

———◇———

EDITED BY

## FREDERICK J. FURNIVALL, M.A.

EDITOR OF 'THE BABEES BOOK, ETC.' ('MANNERS AND MEALS IN OLDEN TIME'),
ETC. ETC.

———

LONDON:
PUBLISHED FOR THE EARLY ENGLISH TEXT SOCIETY,
BY N. TRÜBNER & CO., 60, PATERNOSTER ROW.

———
MDCCCLXVIII.

# PREFACE.

THOUGH no excuse can be needed for including in our Extra Series a reprint of a unique Caxton on a most interesting subject, yet this Book of Curtesye from Hill's MS. was at first intended for our original series, I having forgotten lately that Caxton had written to 'lytyl Iohn,' though some months back I had entered the old printer's book for my second collection of Manners and Meals tracts for the Society. After the copy of Hill—which Mr W. W. King kindly made for his fellow-members—had gone to press, Mr Hazlitt reminded me of the Caxton, and its first and last lines in Mr Blades's admirable book showed that Hill's text was the same as the printed one. I accordingly went to Cambridge to copy it, and there, before tea, Mr Skeat showed me the copy of *The Vision of Piers Plowman* which the Provost and Fellows of Oriel had been good enough to lend him for his edition of 'Text B.' Having enjoyed the vellum Vision, I turned to the paper leaves at its end, and what should they contain but an earlier and better version of the Caxton that I had just copied part of?[1] I drank seven cups of tea, and eat five or six large slices of bread and butter, in honour of the event;[2] and Mr Skeat, with his never-

---

[1] Mr Bradshaw was kind enough to copy the rest, and to read the whole of the proof with Caxton's original.

[2] I must be excused for not having found the poem before, as it is not in the Index to Mr Coxe's Catalogue. In the body of the work it is entered as "A father's advice to his son; with instructions for his behaviour as a king's or nobleman's page. ff. 88, 89, 78. Beg.

Kepeth clene and leseth not youre gere."

failing kindness, undertook to copy and edit the Oriel text for the
Society. With three texts, therefore, in hand, I could not well stick
them at the end of the Postscript to the *Babees Book*, &c.,[1] and as I
wanted Caxton's name to this Book of Curtesye to distinguish it from
what has long been to me THE Book of Courtesy,—that from the
Sloane MS. 1986, edited by Mr Halliwell for the Percy Society, and
by me for our own E. E. T. S.—and as also Caxton's name is one 'to
conjure withal,' I have, with our Committee's leave, made this little
volume an Extra Series one, and called it Caxton's, though his text
is not so good as that of the Oriel MS.

On this latter point Mr Skeat writes :

"The Oriel copy is evidently the best. Not only does it give
better readings, but the lines, as a rule, run more smoothly ; and it
has an extra stanza. This stanza, which is marked 54, occurs
between stanzas 53 and 54 of the other copies, and is of some interest
and importance. It shows that Lidgate's pupil, put in mind of
Lidgate's style by the very mention of his name, introduces a ballad
of three stanzas, in which every stanza has a burden after the Lidgate
manner. The recurrence of this burden no doubt caused copyists to
lose their place, and so the stanza came to be omitted in other copies.
Its omission, however, spoils the ballad. Both it and the curious
lines in Piers Ploughmans Crede,

> For aungells and arcangells · all þei whiȝt vseþ
> And alle aldermen · þat ben *ante tronum*,

i. e. all the elders before the throne, allude to Rev. iv. 10. This Crede
passage has special reference to the *Carmelites* or *White* Friars.

"The first two leaves of the Oriel copy are misplaced inside out at
the end ; but this is not the only misarrangement. The poem has
evidently been copied into this MS. from an older copy having a leaf
capable of containing *six stanzas at a time ;* which leaves were out of
order. Hence the poem in the Oriel MS. is written in the following
order, as now bound up, Stanzas 11 (l. 5)—18, 25—30, 37—42,
19—24, 49—54, 31—36, 43—48, 55—76, 8—11 (l. 4), 4 (l. 5)—7,
1—4 (l. 4)."

---

[1] The Treatises in *The Babees Book*, &c., and the Index at the end, should be
consulted for parallel and illustrative passages to those in Caxton's text.

As an instance of a word improved by the Oriel text, may be cited the '*brecheles* feste' of Caxton's and Hill's texts, l. 66, and l. 300,

> ffor truste ye well ye shall you not excuse
> ffrom *brecheles feste*, & I may you espye
> Playenge at any game of rebawdrye.—*Hill*, l. 299—301.

Could it be 'profitless,' from A.-Sax. *bréc*, gain, profit; or 'breechless,' a feast of birch for the boy with his breeches off? The latter was evidently meant, but it was a forced construction. The Oriel *byrcheley* set matters right at once.

Another passage I cannot feel sure is set at rest by the Oriel text. Hill's and Caxton's texts, when describing the ill-mannered servant whose ways are to be avoided, say of him, as to his hair, that he is

> Absolon with disheveled heres smale,
> lyke to a prysoner of saynt Malowes,[1]
> a *sonny busshe able to the galowes*.—*Hill*, l. 462.

For the last line the Oriel MS. reads,

> a *sonny bush myght cause hym to goo louse*,

and Mr Skeat says,—"This is clearly the right reading, of which *galowes* is an unmeaning corruption. The poet is speaking of the *dirty* state of a bad and ill-behaved servant. He is as dirty as a man come out of St Malo's prison; a sunny bush would cause him to go and free himself from minute attendants. A 'sunny bush' probably means no more than a warm nook, inviting one to rest, or to such quiet pursuits as the one indicated. That this is really the reading is shown by the next stanza, wherein the poet apologizes for having spoken too bluntly; he ought to have spoken of such a chase by saying that he goes *a-hawking* or *a-hunting*. Such was the right euphemism required by 'norture.'"

If this is the meaning, we may compare with it the old poet's reproof to the proud man:

---

[1] An allusion to the strong castle built at St Malo's by Anne, Duchess of Bretayne.—Dyce.

> Man, of þi schuldres and of þi side
> þou miȝte hunti luse and flee :
> of such a park i ne hold no pride ;
> þe dere nis nauȝte þat þou mighte sle.
>
> *Early English Poems*, ed. F. J. F., 1862, p. 1, l. 5.

and remember that one of the blessings of the early Paradisaical *Land of Cokaygne* is :

> Nis þer flei, fle, no lowse,
> In cloþ, in toune, bed, no house.
>
> *Ib.*, p. 157, l. 37-8.

We may also compare the following extract about Homer's death from " Pleasant and Delightfull Dialogues in Spanish and English : Profitable to the Learner, and not vnpleasant to any other Reader. By *John Minsheu*, Professor of Languages in London. 1623," p. 47.

" F ... a foole with his foolishnesse framed in his owne imagination may giue to a hundred wise men matter to picke out.

" I, So it hapned to the Poet Homer, that as he was with age blinde, and went walking by the sea shoare, & heard certaine Fishermen talking, that at that time were a *lowsing* themselues, and as he asked them, what fish they caught, they vnderstanding that he had meant their lice, they answered, Those that we [1] haue, we seeke for, and those that we [2] haue not wee finde, but as the good Homer could not see what they did, and for this cause could not vnderstand the riddle, it did so grieue his vnderstanding to obtaine the secret of this matter, which was a sufficient griefe to cause his death."

But the subject is not a very pleasant one for discussion, though the occupation alluded to in the Oriel Text must have been one of the pastimes of many people in Early England.

The book itself, *Lytill Johan*, is by a disciple of Lydgate's—see l. 366, p. 36-7—and contains, besides, the usual directions how to dress, how to behave in church, at meals, and when serving at table, a wise man's advice on the books his little Jack should read, the best English poets,—then Gower, Chaucer, Occleve, and Lydgate,— not the Catechism and Latin Grammar. It was very pleasant to come

---

[1] i. Haue in their clothes, i. lice.          [2] i. Haue not in hand.

off the directions not to conveye spetell over the table, or burnish une's bones with one's teeth, to the burst of enthusiasm with which the writer speaks of our old poets. He evidently believed in them with all his heart; and it would have been a good thing for England if our educators since had followed his example. If the time wasted, almost, in Latin and Greek by so many middle-class boys, had been given to Milton and Shakspere, Chaucer and Langland, with a fit amount of natural science, we should have been a nobler nation now than we are. There is no more promising sign of the times than the increased attention paid to English in education now.

But to return to our author. He gives Chaucer the poet's highest gift, Imagination, in these words,

> what ever to say he toke in his entente,
> his langage was so fayer & pertynante,
> yt semeth vnto manys heryng
> *not only the worde, but veryly the thyng.* (l. 343.)

And though the writer has the bad taste to praise Lydgate more than Chaucer, yet we may put this down to his love for his old master, and may rest assured that though the cantankerous Ritson calls the Bury schoolmaster a 'driveling monk,' yet the larking schoolboy who robbed orchards, played truant, and generally raised the devil in his early days (*Forewords to Babees Book*, p. xliv.), retained in later years many of the qualities that draw to a man the boy's bright heart, the disciple's fond regret. We too will therefore hope that old Lydgate's

> sowle be gon
> (To) the sterred paleys above the dappled skye,
> Ther to syng *Sanctus* insessavntly
> Emonge the mvses nyne celestyall,
> Before the hyeste Iubyter of all. (l. 381-5.)

In old age the present poem was composed (st. 60, p. 42-3); 'a lytill newe Instruccion' to a lytle childe, to remove him from vice & make him follow virtue. At his riper age our author promises his boy the surplusage of the treatise (st. 74, p. 50-1); and if a copy of it exists, I hope it will soon fall in our way and get into type, for 'the more the merrier' of these peeps into old boy-life.

On one of the grammatical forms of the Oriel MS., Mr Skeat
writes :

"It is curious to observe the forms of the imperative mood plural
which occur so frequently throughout the poem in the Oriel copy. The
forms ending in *-eth* are about 31 in number, of which 17 are of
French, and 14 of A.S. origin. The words in which the ending *-eth*
is dropped are 42, of which 18 are of French, and 24 of A.S. origin.
The three following French words take *both* forms ; *avyse* or *avyseth*,
*awayte* or *awayteth*, *wayte* or *wayteth ;* and the five following A.S.
words, *be* or *beth*, *kepe* or *kepeth*, *knele* or *knelyth*, *loke* or *loketh*,
*make* or *maketh*. Thus the poet makes use, on the whole, of one
form almost as often as the other (that is, supposing the scribe to
have copied correctly), and he no doubt consulted his convenience in
taking that one which suited the line best. It is an instance of what
followed in almost every case of naturalization, that A.S. inflections
were added to the French words quite as freely as to those of native
origin. Both the *-eth* and *-e* forms are commonly used without the
word *ye*, though *Be ye* occurs in l. 58. In the phrase *avise you* (l.
78), *you* is in the accusative."

Commenting also on l. 71 of Caxton and Hill, Mr Skeat notices
how they have individualised the general ' child ' of the earlier Oriel
text :

"71. Here we find *child* riming to *mylde*. In most other places
it is *Johan*. The rime shows that the reading *child* is right, and
*Johan* is a later adaptation. The Oriel MS. never uses the word
*Johan* at all ; it is always *child*."

I may remark also, that on the question lately raised by Mr
Bradshaw, ' who before Hampole,[1] or after him, used *you* for the
nominative as well as the correct *ye*,' Hill uses both *you* and *ye*, see
l. 47, 51, 52, &c., though so far as a hasty search shows, Lydgate, in
his Minor Poems at least, uses *ye* only, as do Lord Berners in his
*Arthur of Lytil Brytayne*, ab. 1530, the Ormulum, Ancren Riwle,
Genesis and Exodus, William of Palerne, Alliterative Poems, Early
Metrical Homilies, &c.[2]

---

[1] *Pricke of Conscience*, p. 127, l. 4659 ; and p. xvii.

[2] Mr Skeat holds that in the various reading ȝow *drieth* from the Univ. Coll.

The final *d*, *f*, *t*, of Hill's MS., often have a tag to them. As they sometimes occur in places where I judge they must mean nothing, I have neglected them all. Every final *ll* has a line through it, which may mean *e*. Nearly every final *n* and *m* has a curly tail or line over it. This is printed *e* or *ñ*, though no doubt the tail and line have often no value at all. The curls to the *rs* are printed *e*, because *ther* with the curly *r*, in l. 521, Hill, rimes to *where* of l. 519.

At the end of Caxton's final *d* and *g* is occasionally a crook-backed line, something between the line of beauty and the ordinary knocker. This no doubt represents the final *e* of MSS., and is so printed, as Mr Childs has not the knocker in the fount of type that he uses for the Society's work. Caxton's *ñ* stands for *un* in the *-aunce*, *-aunte*, of words from the French. No stops or inverted commas have been put to Caxton's text here, but the stanzas and lines have been numbered, and side-notes added.

" The *Book of Curtesye*," says Mr Bradshaw, " is known from three early editions. The first, without any imprint, but printed at Westminster by Caxton ab. 1477-78,[1] the only known copy of which is here reproduced. The second (with the colophon 'Here endeth a lytyll treatyse called the booke of Curtesye' or lytyll John. Emprynted atte Westmoster') is only known from a printer's proof of two pages[2] preserved among the Douce fragments in the Bodleian. It must have been printed by Wynkin de Worde in Caxton's house ab. 1492. In the third edition it was reprinted at the end of the *Stans puer ad Mensam* by Wynkin de Worde ab. 1501-1510. The Cambridge copy is the only one known to remain of this edition."

I have no more to say: but, readers, remember this coming New Year to do more than last for what Dr Stratmann calls "the dear Old English." Think of Chaucer when his glad spring comes, and

Oxford MS. (of the early part of the 15th century) to the Vernon MS. *þou druȝest*, l. 25, Passus 1, of the Vision of Piers Plowman, the ȝow is an accusative, " exactly equivalent to the Gothic in the following passage—' *hwana* þaursjai, gaggai du mis, i. e. *whom* it may thirst, let him come to me.' John vii. 37. I conclude that ȝow is accusative, not dative. The same construction occurs in German constantly, ' *es dürstet mich* ' == it thirsts me, I thirst."

[1] In his type No. 2, *Blades*, ii. 63.
[2] In Caxton's type No. 5, *Blades*, ii. 235 (not 253 as in Index).

every day besides ; forget not Langland or any of our early men ;

reporte

 & revyue *the* lawde of the*m* that were
 famovs in[1] owre langage, these faders dere,
  whos sowles i*n* blis, god ete*r*nall avaunce,
  *tha*t lysten so[2] owre langage to enhavnce !

(*Hill*, 1. 430-4.)

3, *St George's Square, N.W.*
 15 *Dec.*, 1867.

---

[1] Founders of, *Oriel* MS.      [2] some, *Hill ;* so, *Oriel.*

# The Book of Curtesye.

# [The Book of Curtesy.]

*[From the Oriel MS. lxxix.]*

### [1]

Lytle childe, sythen youre tendre infancie
Stondeth as yett vndir yndyff[e]rence,
To vice or vertu to moven [1] or Applie,      3  ¹ MS. morven.
  And in suche Age ther is no prouidence,
  Ne comenly no sadde intelligence,
    But ryght as wax receyueth printe and figure,
    So chylder ben disposed of nature,

### [2]

Vice or vertu to Folowe and ympresse
  In mynde ; and therfore, to stere and remeve
You from vice, and to vertu thou² dresse,      10  ² Read you.
  That on to folow, and the other to eschewe,
  I haue devysed you this lytill newe
    Instruccion according to youre age,
    Playne in sentence, but playner in langage.   14

---

*(Richard Hill's Commonplace Book, or Balliol MS. 354, ffl C lx.)*

Here begynnyth lytill Iohan.

Lytell Iohan, sith your tendere enfancye     [Hill's Text.]
  Stondyth as yet vndere Indyfference
To vyce or vertu to mevyn or applie,
4   & in suche age ther [1] ys no provydence,
  Ne comenly no sage Intelygence,
    But as wax receyvith prynt or fygure,
    So chyldren bene disposed of nature

   ¹ The *th* is the same as the *y*.

# [The Book of Curtesye.]

[*Caxton's Text.*]

### [1]

Stondeth as yet vnder / in difference

To vice or vertu to meuyn or applye

And in suche age ther is no prouidence

Ne comenly no sade Intelligence

But as waxe resseyueth prynte or figure

So children ben disposide of nature     7

*right margin:* [Leaf 1 a.] As Infancy is indifferent whether it follows vice or virtue,   **3**

### [2]

Vyce or vertue to folowe ande enpresse   ▼

In mynde / ande therfore / to styre & remeue

You from vice / ande to vertue addresse   10

That one to folowe / and that other teschewe

I haue deuysed you / this lytyl newe

Instruccion / acordynge vnto your age

Playne in sentence / but playner in langage   14

*right margin:* I have written this new treatise to draw you from vice, and turn you to virtue.

---

¶ Vyce or vertu to folowe, & enpresse

In mynde ; & therfor to styre & remeve

you frome vice, & to vertu addresse,

That on to folow, & that other to eschewe,

I haue devysed you this lytill newe

Instruccion [1] accordyng vnto your age,

playn In sentence, but playnere In langage.

*right margin:* [*Hill's Text.*]

[1] The mark of contraction is over the *n* : t. i. the *n* has its tail curled over its back like a dog's.

[3]

Taketh hede therfore and herkyn what I say,
  And yeueth therto hooly youre aduertence,
Lette not youre eye be here and youre hert away,        17
  But yeueth herto youre besy diligence,
  And ley aparte alle wantawne insolence,
    Lernyth to be vertues and well thewid ;
    Who wolle not lere, nedely must be lewid.          21

[4]

Afore all thyng, fyrst and principally,
  In the morowe when ye¹ shall vppe ryse,              ¹ MS. he.
To wyrship god haue in youre memorie ;                 24
  Wyth cristis erosse loke ye blesse you thriese,
  Youre pater-nosteir seyth in devoute wyse,
    Aue maria wyth the holy crede,
    Than alle the after the bettir may ye spede.       28

[5]

And while ye be Abouten honestely
  To dresse youre-self and don on youre aray,
Wyth youre felawe well and tretably                    31
  Oure lady matens Avyseth that you say,
  And this obseruaunce vseth euery day,
    Wyth prime and owris, and wythouten drede
    The blyssed lady woll graunte you youre mede.  35

---

  ¶ Take hede therfor, & harken what I saye,           [Hill's Text.]
16      & geve therto yowre good advertence,
      lette not your ere be here, & your herte awaye,
      But pute you therto besy delygence,
      Laying a-parte all wanton Insolence,
20      lernyd to be vertuvs & well thewed ;
      who will not lerne, nedely he must be lewed.

  ¶ Afore all thyng, & pryncypally
      In the mornyng whan ye vp ryse,
24    To worship god haue in memory ;
      with crystis crosse loke ye blesse ye thryse,

[3]

Take hede therfore / and herkne what I saye
Ande gyue therto / your goode aduertence
Lete not your ere be here & your herte awaye　17
But put ye therto / besy diligence
Leynge aparte al wantown Insolence
Lerneth to be vertuous / and wel thewede
Who wil not lerne / nedely he must be lewed　21

Attend therefore to what I say.

Learn good manners.

[4]

Afore alle thinge / ande principally
In the morenynge / whan ye vp rise
To worshipe gode / haue in memorie　24
With crystes crosse / loke ye blesse you thrise
Your pater noster / saye in deuoute wyse
Aue maria / with the holy crede
Thenne alle the day / the better shal ye spede　28

[Leaf 1 b.]

On rising,

cross yourself,

say your Pater Noster, Ave, and Creed.

[5]

And while that ye be aboute honestly
To dresse your self / & do oñ your araye
With your felawe / wel and tretably　31
Oure lady matyns / loke that ye saye
Ande this obseruañce / vse ye every daye
With pryme and ouris / withouten drede
The blesside lady / wil qnyte you your mede　35

While dressing,

say our Lady's Matins,

Prime, and Hours.

---

[Hill's Text.]

　　your patere noster say in devoute wyse,
　　　Aue maria / with the holy crede ;
28　　Then aꝉ the day the better shall ye spede.

　¶ And while ye dresse your selfe, honestly
　　　To dresse your selfe & do on your araye,
　　with your felowe weꝉ & tretably
32　　Owre lady matens loke that you say ;
　　And this observance vse ye euery day,
　　　with pryme & owers with-owt drede.
　　the blessyd lady wiꝉ quyte you your mede.

2

[6]

Kembe youre hede and loke ye kepe hit clene,
    Youre eris twayne suffre not foule to be ;
In youre visage wayteth no spotte be sene,          38
    Purge youre nase, let hit not combred be
Wyth foule matiers Ayenst all oneste,
        But wyth bare hande no matier from hit feche,
        For that is a foule and an vncurtays teche.          42

[7]

Youre handes wassheth, that is an holsom thyng,
    Youre nayles loke they be not geet blake,
Suffre hem not to ben ouer long growyng ;          45
    To youre aray good hede I warne you take,
    That manerly ye seet hit vp and make,
        Youre hode, youre gowne, youre hose, and eke
            youre scho,
        Wyth all array longyng youre body to.          49

[8]

Kepeth clene and leseth not youre gere,
    And or ye passen oute of youre loggyng,
Euery garment that ye schulle vppon you were,          52
    Awayteth welle that hit be so syttyng
As to youre degre semeth moost on accordyng ;
        Than woll men sey, ' for soth this childe is he
        That is well taught and loueth honeste.'          56

---

36 ¶ Kembe your hede, & loke you kepe yt clene ;          [Hill's Text.]
        your eres twayn suffre not fowle to be ;          [m C lx back]
        In your wysage loke no spote be sene ;
        purge your nose ; lett no man in yt se
    40  The vile matter ; yt ys none honeste ;
        Ne with your bare hond no fylth from yt feche,
        ffor that ys fowle, & an vncurtoys teche.

    ¶ Your hondis wasshe ; yt ys an holsom thyng ;
    44  your naylis loke they be not gety blake,
        Ne suffre not them over longe growyng.

### [6]

Kembe your hede / & loke ye kepe it clene

Your eres tweyne / suffre not fowl to be

In your visage / wayte no spot be sene — 38

Purge your nose / lete noman in it see

The vile mater / it is none honeste

Ne with your bare honde / no filth fro it fecche

For that is fowl / and an vncurtoys teche — 42

Comb your head; clean your ears

and nose;

don't pick it.

### [7]

Your hondes wesshe / it is an holsom thing*e*

Your naylis loke / they be not gety blacke

Ne suffre not hem / to be *o*uer longe growyng — 45

To your araye / I warne you good hede take

That manerly ye fytte it vp and make

Your hood*e*. gowne. hosyn / & eke your sho

With al your aray longyng your body to — 49

[Leaf 2 a.] Wash your hands; don't keep your nails jet-black or too long.

Wear fit clothes, that fit well

### [8]

Kepe you clene / and lose not your gere

And or ye passe / out of your loggyng*e*

Euery garment / that ye shal on were — 52

Awayte wel / that it be so syttyng*e*

As to your degre / semeth acordyng*e*

Then*n*e wil men saye / forsoth this childe is he

That is wel taught / and louyth honeste — 56

and suit your station;

the men will praise you.

---

To yo*ur* A-raye I warne you good hede take,
Manerly & ffyte loke you yt make;
48    yo*ur* hood / gown*e* / hosen / & eke your sho,
wi*th* all yo*ur* araye longyng yo*ur* body to.

¶ Kepe you clene, & lose not yo*ur* gere;
& or you passe owt of yo*ur* lodgyng,
52    Eu*er*y garment *that* ye shall were,
Awayte well *that* yt be so syttyng
& to yo*ur* degre semed acordyng;
Tha*n* will me*n* say, " for sothe *th*is child ys he
56    *that* ys well tawght, & loweth honeste."

[*Hill's Text.*]

2 *

[9]

And as ye walke and passen be the strete,
Be ye not nyce of chere and countenance ;
And loke, my childe, to folkys that ye mete,          59
Ye spekyn feyre wyth wordis of plesaunce ;
To youre souerayne wyth humble obeysaunce,
To hym that is youre felowe and pere,
Yevith feyre langage wyth ryght frendly chere. 63

[10]

CAst not wyth stone or styke at foule ne beste,
And where ye walke be ware that ye ne rage,[1]      [1] MS. nerage.
For and ye do, ye shall to byrcheley feest.          66
Terre[2] wyth no hounde in fylde nor in village,     [2] MS. There, by mistake.
Gothe forth in peace, demenyng youre vysage
In sobre wyse, that men may of you say,
' A goodly childe ther passith be the way.'          70

[11]

Whan ye come to the chirche, my lytyll chylde,
Holy watir ye schull vppon you caste              72
Be-fore the crosse wyth [chere] moste meke and mylde ;
Than knelyth doune and knoketh on youre breste,
Thankyng the lorde that on the crosse did rest,
And there for you suffred his hert to blede,
Seyth or ye ryse Pater, Aue, and A crede.           77

---

¶ And as ye walke & passe by the strete,          [Hill's Text.]
Be ye not Nyce of chere & covntenavnce,
but loke, my child, to folkis that you mete,
60      & loke ye speke fayere with wordis of plesavnce,
Demvre, & curtoys of your Demenavnce.
To hym that ys yowre felow & pere,
Geve you fayre langage & a ffrendly chere.

64 ¶ Cast no styke ne stone at fowle ne beste ;
& wher ye walke, be ware ye ne rage,
ffor yff ye do ye shalt to brecheles feest.
Terre not with hovndis in fyld ne in vilage ;

[9]

And as ye walke / and passe by the strete

Be ye not nyce of chere / and countenaunce

But loke my child / to folkes that ye mete      59

Ye speke fayr / with wordes of plesaunce

Demure and curtoys / of your demenaunce

To hym that is your felawe and*e* pere

Gyue ye fair langage / and a frendly chere      63

*As you walk, look pleasantly at folk,*

*and greet your fellows friendly;*

[10]

Caste no styck ne stone at fowle ne beest

And where ye walke / bewarre ye ne rage

For yf ye doo / ye shal to brecheles feest      66

Terre not with hou*n*de in felde ne in vilage

Go forth your waye / demenyng your viage

In sobre wyse / that men may of you saye

A goodly chyld*e* / ther passeth by the waye      70

*[Leaf 2 b.] don't shy stones at bird or beast,*

*or quarrel with dogs.*

[11]

And whan ye come to þᵉ chirche my litil child

Holy water / ye shal vpon you caste

Byfore þᵉ crosse / with chere meke & myld*e*      73

Knele adoun / and knocke on your breste

Thankyng the good lord þᵗ on it did*e* reste

And there / for you suffryd his sides to blede

Saye ye or ye rise / pat*er* noster / aue / & a crede      77

*At church, holy-water yourself,*

*kneel before the cross, knock on your breast,*

*and say prayers.*

---

68     Go furth yo*ur* way, Demenyng yo*ur* viage      *[Hill's Text.]*

        In sober wyse, *tha*t me*n* maye of you saye,

        " A goodly chyld ther passith by the way."

¶ And whe*n* ye cu*m* to *the* churche, my litill child,

72     holy water ye shall vpon you caste.

        be-fore *the* crosse wi*th* chere meke & myld*e*

        knele a-down*e*, & knoke on yo*ur* brest,

        Thankyng *that* good lord *that* on yt dyde reste,

76     & .ther for you suffred his sydys to blede ;

        Saye ye, or you ryse, pater n*os*ter / aue / & a crede.

### [12]

A vise you well Also for eny thyng,  
  The schirche of prayer is the house and place ;  
Be ware there-fore of clappe or Ianglyng,       80  
  For in the schirche that is full gret trysspace,  
  And A token of hem that lacken grace ;  
    Ther beth demure and kepeth youre sylence,  
    And serueth god wyth all youre deligence.      84

### [13]

To helpe the prest whan he shall sey the masse,  
  Whan hit shall happen you or be-tyde,  
Remeue not ferre ne from his presence passe,      87  
  Kneleth or stondeth deuoutly hym be-syde,  
  And not to nyghe ; youre tounge mooste be applied  
    To Answere hym wyth [1] v[o]ice full moderate ;    [1] MS. wyth hym wyth.  
    Avÿse you well, my lityll childe, Algate      91

### [14]

To mynystre wyth de-voute Reuerence,  
  Loke that ye do youre humble obseruaunce  
Debonarly wyth [dewe] obideence,      94  
  Cyrcum-spectly, wyth euer[y] circumstaunce  
  Of porte, of chere, demevire of countenaunce,  
    Remembryng, the lord aboue is he  
    Whom to serue is grettest liberte.      98

---

¶ Avyce you well also for any thynge,      [Hill's Text.]  
  The chyrche, of prayer ys howse & place ;  
80   be ware therfor of clappe or Iangelynge,  
  ffor in the chyrche yt ys a full gret trespas,  
  & a token of suche as lacketh grace.  
  Ther be ye demvre, & kepe ye scilence,  
84   And serve ye god with all your delygence.

  To helpe the Preest whan he sayth masse,      [fi C lxj.]  
  whan yt shall happen you or betyde,  
  Remeve not fer, ne from his presence passe ;  
88   knele or stonde you devovtly hym besyde,

### [12]

Auyse you wel also / for ony thinge
The chirche of prayer / is hous and place
Beware therfore / of clappe or Iangelynge     80   Don't chatter,
For in þᵉ chirche / it is a ful grete trespaas
And a token of suche / as lackyth grace
There be ye demure / and kepe ye scilence       but be silent, and
                                             serve God.
And serue ye god / with al your diligence     84

### [13]

To helpe the preest / whan he saith masse         [Leaf 3 a.]
                                              When you help
Whan it shal happen you or betyde             the priest at
                                              Mass,
Remeue not fer / ne from his presence passe    87
Knele or stonde ye / deuoutly hym besyde      kneel or stand
                                              near him,
And not to nygh your tonge muste be applide
Tanswere hym / with voys ful moderate       and answer him
                                              in a moderate
Auyse you wel / my lityl childe algate       91   tone.

### [14]

To mynystre / with deuoute reuerence        Minister
Loke ye do / youre humble obseruañce        reverently
Debonairly / with due obedyence             94
Circumspectly / with euery circumstaunce      and circum-
                                              spectly.
Of poort and chere / of goodly countenañce
Remembrynge wel the lorde / a boue is he
Whom to serue / is grettest liberte          98

---

       & not to nygh : your tonge mvst be applyde     [Hill's Text.]
         To answere hym with woyce moderate.
         Avyce you well, my lytiłł child, algate

92 ¶ To mynyster with devout reverence ;
       loke ye do your humble observaunce
       Debonerly wyth dewe obedyence,
       Circumspectly with euery circumstavnce
96    Of poort, & chere of goodly covntenavnce,
       Remembryng well the lorde a-bove ys he,
       whome to serve ys grettest lyberte.

### [15]

And whan ye speke, loketh men in the face [1]
  Wyth sobre chere and goodly semblaunce;
Cast not youre eye asyde in odir place,      101
  For that is a tokyn of wantowne inconstaunce,
  Which wolle appeyre youre name, and disauaunce;
    The wyse man seyth, 'who hathe this signes thre
    Ne is not like a good man [for] to be—     105

1 MS. visage.

### [16]

Yn hert,' he seyth, 'who that is inconstaunte,[2]
  A waveryng eye, glyddryng but sodenly
From place to place, and A fote [3] variaunte [4]    108
  That in no place abydeth stabully—
  Thes ben signes,' the wyse man seyth sekerly,
    'Of suche a wyght as is vnmanerly nyce,
    And is full like dissposed be to vice.'     112

2 MS. inconstaunce

3 MS. fore.
4 MS. variaunce.

### [17]

And wayte, my childe, whan ye stond at the table,
  Of souereyne or maister whether hit be,
Applieth you [for] to be seruysable,      115
  That no defaute in you may founde be;
  Loke who doth best and hym envyeth ye,
    And specially vseth attendaunce,
    Whiche is to souereyne thyng of gret plesaunce. 119

---

¶ And whan ye speke, loke men in the face
100    with sobre chere & goodly semblavnce;
     Caste not eye a-side in no othere place,
     ffor that ys a token of a wanton constavnce,
     which will apayre your name, & dysavance.
104     The wyse man sayth, 'who hath these thyngis iij,
     ys not lyke a good man for to be:

¶ 'In herte,' he sayth, 'who that ys Inconstavnte,
     A waverynge eye, glydyng sodenly
108   ffro place to place, & a foote varyavnte
     that in no place a-bydyth stabli,

[Hill's Text.]

### [15]

And whan ye speke / loke men in the face
With sobre chere / ande goodly semblaunce
Caste not your eye a syde / in other place    ·    101
For that is a token of wantouñ inconstance
Whiche wil appeyre your name & disauañce
The wise man saith who hath these thingis thre
Is not lyke a goode man for to be     105

When you speak to men, look 'em in the face.

The Wise Man says

### [16]

In herte he seith / who that is inconstañte
A waueryng eye / glydyng sodeynly
Fro place to place / & a foot variañte    108
That in no place / abydeth stably
These ben þᵉ signes / the wiseman seith sikerly
Of suche a wight / as is vnmanerly nyce
And is ful likely disposid vnto vyce    112

[Leaf 3 b.]

an inconstant man with a wavering eye and a wandering foot

will turn to vice.

### [17]

Awayte my chylde / whan ye stande atte table
Of maister or souerayn / whether it be
Applye you for to be seruysable    .    115
That no defaute in you founden be
Loke / who doth best / and hym ensiewe ye
And in especyal / vse ye attendaunce
Wherein ye shal your self best auaunce    119

When you serve at table,

be attentive and ndy,

specially to well-off men.

---

Thyse bene *the* thyng*is*,' *the* wysman sayth   [*Hill's Text.*]
    sekerly,
      ' Off suche a wayghte *that* be vnmanerly nyce,
112     & be full lykely dysposed vnto vyce.'

¶ Awayte, my chyld, whan ye stonde at table,
    Off mayster or soverayne whe*ther* yt be,
    Applye you for to be servysable
116     That no defawte in you fownden be ;
    loke who dothe best, & hym folow ye,
    & in especyall vse ye attendavnce
    wheryn ye shall your selfe best avaunce.

[18]

A [s] ye be comaundyd, so ye do algate,
   Beth not wyth-oute cause from the tabul absent ;
Hit is plesaunce vnto the gret astate          122
   To se theyre saruaunt about them present ;
   Haunteth no halkes, for then ye woll be schent.
      Lette maner and Mesure be youre guydes twey,
      So shall ye best please, I dare well sey.      126

[19]

R ewarde all-way the loke and countenaunce
   Of youre master, or of youre souereine,
Ther shall ye best preue what is plesaunce,      129
   And what displesaunce ; this is the soth serteyne,
   The chere discureth often tyme both twayne,
      And eke the chere may some tyme you addresse
      In thyng that langage may not þan expresse.   133

[20]

A nd what ye here there, loke ye kepe hit secre,
   Besy report of mystrust is cheff norice ;
Mekell langage may not all fautles be ;          136
   Than doth, my childe, as teicheth you the wyse,
   Whiche vnto you this wysdome dothe devise,
      ' Here and see, be still in euery prees,[1]
      Passe forth youre way in silence and in pees.'

1 MS. 'in euery place and in prees.' *Place* was to have been the last word ; *and in prees* was carelessly *added*, instead of striking out *place*.—Sk.

---

120 ¶ As ye be comavnded, so do ye algate ;
         be not cavseles fro *the* table absente ;
         yt ys a grete pleasure to *the* high estate [1]
         To se his servaunttes abowte hym presente.
124      havnte no halke, for the*n* ye wiłł be shente ;
         lette manere & mesure be yo*ur* gydes twayne ;
         so shałł ye best please, I dare savely sayne.

¶ Reward also thy loke & contenavnce,
128      Off your master or of your soverayne,
         so shałł ye best preve what ys his plesavnce
         or ellis his dysplesavnce : this ys sertayne,

[*Hill' s Text.*]

[1 noble, lord.]

## [18]

As ye be comandede / so do ye algate  
Be not causeles / fro the table absent  
It is a grete plesure / to the hyghe estate     122  
To see his seruantis aboute hym present  
Haunte no halke / for thenne ye wil be shente  
Lete maner & mesure / be your gydes tweyne  
So shal ye best plese / I dar sauely seyne     126

Don't absent yourself from table,

or stick yourself in a corner. Let Manners and Moderation guide you.

## [19]

Rewarde also the loke ande contenaunce  
Of your maister / or of your souereyne  
So shal ye best preue. what is his plesañce     129  
Or els displesaunce / this is soth serteyne  
The chere discouerith / often bothe tweyne  
And eke þᵉ chere / somtyme may you addresse  
In thingis / þᵗ langage may not them expresse     133

[Leaf 4 a.] Look at your master's face; that'll show whether he's pleased or not.

## [20]

Ande that ye her loke / kepe alway secree  
Besy reporte / of mischief is chief noryse  
Mykyl langage / may not al fawtles bee     136  
Thenne do my childe / as techeth you the wyse  
Whiche vnto you / this lesson doth deuyse  
Here and see / ande be stylle in euery prees  
Passe forth your way in scilence & in pees     140

Keep secret all you hear.

Hear, see, and go your way.

---

132     The chere discovereth oftyn both[e] twayn,  
      & eke the chere sumtyme may yow addresse  
      In thyngis the langage may not then expresse.

[Hill's Text.]

¶ .And that ye here, loke ye kepe alway secre ;  
      besy reporte, of myschefe ys chefe noryse ;  
136     Mykyll langage may not all fawtles be ;  
      Then do, my chyld, as techeth you the wyse  
      whiche vnto you this lessun doth devyce :  
      here & see, & be styll in euery prees,  
140     passe forthe your way in scilence & in pees.

[fll C lxj, back.]

### [21]

And yit in Aventure ye, if the caase require,
  Ye most speke as hit may doo percace ; [1]           [1] MS. precace.
Seuen condicions obserue as ye shall hire,       143
  Avise you well what ye sey and in what place,
  Of whom, and to whom, in youre mynde compace ;
    Howe ye shall speke, and whan, taketh good hede,
    This counseilleth the wyse man wyth-outen drede.

### [22]

Awayte, my childe, ye haue you manerly,
  Whan at youre mete ye sittyn at youre table ;
In euery pres, in euery company,       150
  Disposeth you to be so componable,
  That men may you reporte for comendable ;
    For tristeth well, vppon youre bering
    Men woll you blame or yeven you preysing.    154

### [23]

And printeth chiefly in youre memorie,
  For A principalle poynt of feire norture,
Ye depraue no man absent especially ;       157
  Seint Austyn Amonishith wyth besy cure,
  Howe at the table men shull them assure,
    That there escapeth them no suche langage,
    As myght turne other folke to disparage.    161

---

¶ And yet in aduenture, yf the caas requyre,     [Hill's Text.]
  ye may speke, but ye must percaas
  Seven [1] condycions obserue, as ye may here :    [1 Six they are at
144   Avyce ye well what ye say, & in what place,    p. 358, Babees
  Off whom, & to whom, in your mynd compace ;   Book, of the Wise
  how ye shall speke, & whan, take good hede :   Man.]
  this cow[n]syled the wyse man withowten
  drede.

148   A-wayte, my chyld, ye behaue you manerly
  whan at your mete ye sytte at the table ;
  In euery prees & In euery cumpany

## [21]

And yet in auenture / yf the caas require
Ye may speke / but ye muste thenne *percaas*
Seue*n* *condicions* obserue / as ye may now hyre   143
Auyse you wel / what ye saye / & in what place
Of whom / & to whom in your mynde co*m*pace
How ye shal speke / & whan take good hede
This cou*n*celith the wise man withoute drede   147

If you must speak, observe the seven conditions.

## [22]

Awayte my chylde / ye be haue you manerly
Whan at your mete / ye sitte at the table
In euery prees and in euery company   150
Dispose you to be so compenable
That men may of you reporte for *commendable*
For trusteth wel / vpon your berynge
Men wil you blame or gyue preysynge   154

[Leaf 4 b.]

When you're at meals,

be companionable

## [23]

And prynte ye trewly your memorie
For a princypal point of fair noreture
Ye depraue no man absent especyally   157
Saynt austyn amonessheth with besy cure
How men atte table / shold hem assure
That there escape them / no suche langage
As myght other folke hurte to disparage   161

and don't run down absent men. St Austin

---

[Hill's Text.]

152   Dyspose you to be so cu*m*penable
    *th*at me*n* may of you reporte for *commendable*;
    ffor, trustyth well, vpon yo*ur* beryng
    Men will you blame or gyve *praysyng.

¶ And prynte ye truly *th*is in yo*ur* memorye
156   for a pryncypall poynt of fayer noretvre,
    *th*at ye deprave no ma*n* absente specyally.
    Saynt Austyne amonessheth wi*th* besy cure,
    howe me*n* att table shulde the*m* assure
160   *th*at *th*er escape the*m* no suche langage
    As myght hurte or bryng folke to disparage.

## [24]

This curteise clarke writeth in ryght this wyse,
  Rebukyng the vice of vile detraccioun ;
'What man hit be that of custome and guise      164
  Hurteth wyth his toung wyth foule corrosioun
  The absent wight, for that abusioun
    Suche detractoure [wayue]¹ from this table      ¹ A word lost.
    As vn-worthe, not to be reprocheable.      168 .

## [25]

Whan ye sitten therfor at youre repaste,
  Annoyethe no man present nor absent,
But speketh feyre, for and ye make waste      171
  Off [large] langage, for soth ye·most be schent ;
  And wan ye speke, speketh wyth good entent
    Of maters appendyng to myrth and plesaunce,
    But nothyng that may causen men greuaunce.  175

## [26]

Eschewe also taches of foule rauenyng,
  Of gredy lust the vncurteyce appetite ;
Pres not to sone to youre viaunde, restraine      178
  Youre handis a while wyth manerly respytte ;
  Fedith for necessite, not for delite,
    Demeneth you in mete and drink soo sobrely,
    That ye be not infecte wyth gloteny.      182

---

¶ This curteys clerke wryteth in this wyse,      [Hill's Text.]
    Rebukyng the vyce of vyle detraccion :
164    what may yt be that of custum & gvyse
      hurteth with tonge or by fowle colusyon
      The absente / weyne¹ ye for that abusyon      [¹ or weyue]
      Suche a detractowre from the table
168      As vnworthy & also reprocheable.

¶ Whan ye sytte therfor at your repast,      ·
    Annoye ye no man present nor absente,
    but speke ye fewe ; for yff ye make wast
172    of large langage, for soth ye must be shent.

[24]

This curtoys clerk / writeth in this wise

Rebukynge the vice / of vyle detraccion · · · · · · · · · rebukes the vice of detraction,

What man it be / that of custom & guyse · · · · 164

Hurteth with tunge / or by foule colusiön · · · · and bids you turn all backbiters from the table

Thabsente / weyue ye for that abusioñ

Suche a detractour / from the table

As vnworthy / and also reprochable · · · · · · 168

[25]

Whan ye sitte therfore at your repaste · · · · [Leaf 5 a.]

Annoye ye noman presente nor absente

But speke ye fewe / for yf ye make waste · · · · 171 Speak little,

Of large langage / for sothe ye must be shent

And whan ye speke / speke ye with good entent · · · and that pleasantly.

Of maters acordynge vnto plesance

But nothing / that may cause men greuañce · · · · 175

[26]

Eschewe also tacches of foule Raueyne · · · · · Don't be ravenous,

Of gredy luste / with vncurteys appetyte [1]

Prece not to sone / fro your viand restreyne · · · 178 but keep your hands from your food for a time.

Your honde a while / with manerly respite

Fede you for necessite / & not for delite

Demene you with mete / & drynke so sobrely

That ye not ben enfecte with glotony · · · · · 182

[1] *Orig.* appetyce.

---

& whan ye speke // speke with good Intent

Off maters accordyng vnto plesavnce,

but no thynge that may cavse men grevaunce.

¶ Eschewe also tacches of fowle ravayne,

177   of gredy luste ; with vncurteys appetyte

prece not to sone ; fro your vyande restrayne

your hand a while with manerly respyte ;

180   ffede you for necessyte, & not for delyte.

Demene you with mete & drynke so soberly

That ye not be Infecte wyth glotony.

[27]

Embrewe not youre vesselle ne youre cuppe [1]
  Ouer mesure and maner, but saue them clene ;
Ensoyle not youre cuppe, but kepe hit clenely,   185
  Lete no fatte ferthyng of youre lippe be sen.
  For that is foule ; wotte you what I mene ?
    Or than ye drincke, for youre owne honeste,
    Youre lippis wepe, and klenly loke they be.   189

[1] *Sic.* Read "napery."

[28]

Blowe not in youre drincke ne in youre potage,
  Ne farsith not youre disshe to full of brede,
Ne bere not youre knyf towarde youre vysage,   192
  For there-in is parell and mekell drede.
  Clawe not youre face ne touche not youre hede
    Wyth youre bare hande, sittyng at the table,
    For in norture that is reprouable.   196

[29]

Lowse not youre gyrdyll syttyng at youre table,[2]
  For that is a tache of vncurtesye,
But and ye seme ye be enbrasyde streite,   199
  Or than ye sitte amende hit secrely,
  So couertly that no wyght hit espie.
    Be ware also no breth from you rebounde
    Vppe ne downe, be ware that shamefull sounde.

[2] *Sic.* Read "mete."

---

¶ Enbrewe not your vessell ne your naprye
184   over maner & mesure, but kepe them clene ;
  Ensoyle not your cuppe, but kepe yt clenly,
  lete no farsyone on your lyppis be sene,
  ffor *that* ys fowle ; ye wott what I mene.
188   Or than ye drynke, for your own honeste
  your lyppys wype, & clenly loke they be.

¶ Blowe not in your drynke ne in your pottage,
  Ne ferce not your disshe to full of brede ;
192  bere not your knyf toward your vysage,
  ffor *ther*yn ys peryll & mykell drede ;

[*Hill's Text.*]
[ffl C lxij.]

[27]

Enbrewe not your vessel / ne your naprye

Ouer maner & mesure / but kepe hem clene

Ensoyle not your cuppe / but kepe it clenlye          185

Lete no fat farssine / on your lippes be sene

For that is fowle / ye wote what I mene

Or than ye drynke / for your owen honeste

Your lippes wype / and clenly loke they be           189

*Don't dirty your cloth or cup.*

*Wipe your lips before you drink.*

[28]

Blowe not in your drinke ne in your potage

Ne farse not your dishe to ful of brede

Bere not your knyf / to warde your visage            192

For therin is parelle / and mykyl drede

Clawe not your visage / touche not your hede

With your bare honde / sittyng atte table

For in norture / suche thing is reprouable           196

*[Leaf b b.] Don't blow on your food,*

*or put your knife to your face,*

*or scratch it or your head.*

[29]

Lose not your gyrdel / sittyng at your mete

For that is a tacche / of vncurtesye

But yf ye seme / ye be embraced streite              199

Or then ye sytte / amende it secretly

So couertly that no wight you espye

Beware also / no breth fro you rebounde

Vp ne douñ / leste ye were shameful founde           203

*Don't undo your girdle at table;*

*If it's tight, let it out before you sit down.*

*Don't break wind up or down.*

---

Clawe not your visage, tovche not your hede          *[Hill's Text.]*

    with your bare honde syttyng at the table,

196    ffor in norture suche thyngis be reproveable.

¶ Lose not your gyrdyll syttyng at your mete,

    ffor that is a tache of vncurtesye ;

    but yff ye seme ye be enbrased streyte,

200    or than ye sytte, amend yt secretly

    So wysely that no wyght you aspye.

    be ware also no breth fro you rebownd

    Vp ne downe, lest ye were shamfull fownd.

3

[30]

Beth huste in chambre, cilent in the halle,
  Herkenyth well, yeueth good audience ;
Yef vsher or marchall for eny romour calle,        206
  Putting Ianglers to rebuke and cilence,
  Beth mylde of langage, demure of eloquence ;
    Enforcith you to them confourmyde be,
    That can most good and haue humanyte.      ·210

[31]

Touche not wyth mete salt in the saler,
  Lest folke Appoynt you of vncunnyngnesse,
Dresse hit apparte vppon a clene tranchere ;        213
  Force not youre mouth to fulle for wantannesse,
  Lene not vppon the table, that is but rudesse,
    And yf I shall to you so playnly say,
    Ouer the table ye shull not spette convey.      217

[32]

Yif ye be seruid wyth metis delicate,
  Departith wyth youre fellowys in gentyl wyse,
The clarke seith, ' nature is content and saciate      220
  Wyth meane diete, and lytill shall suffice.'
  Departyth therfore, as I to you devise ;
    Engrosith not vnto youre silven all,
    For gentilnesse will ay be lyberall.      224

---

¶ Be ye husht in chambre, scylente in hall ;
205    herkyn well, & geve good audyence
      yff vsshar or marchall for any rvmowre call ;
      putt ye yanglers to rebuke for scilence.
208    Be ye myld of langage, demvre of eloquence ;
        Enforce you vnto hym conformed to be
        that can most good, & hathe humanyte.

¶ Towch not with your mete salte in the saler,
212    leest folke apoynte you of vnconnyngnesse ;
      Dresse yt aparte vpon a clene trenshere.
      ffarste not your movth to full for wantonesse ;

[30]

Be ye husht in chambre / scylent in halle — Be silent,
Herken wel ande gyue goode audience
Yf vssher or marchal for ony Rumour calle — 206
Put ye Ianglers to rebuke for silence — and put chatterers to rebuke.
Be ye mylde of langage / demure of eloquence
Enforce you vnto hym conformed to be — Imitate him who has humanity.
That can moste good / ande hath humanyte — 210

[31]

Touche not with your mete / salt in the saler — [Leaf 6 a.] Don't dip your meat in the saltcellar,
Lest folk apoynte you of vnconnyngnesse
Dresse it aparte / vpon a clene trencher — 213
Farse not your mouth to ful / for wantonesse
Lene not vpon the table / for that rude is — lean on the table,
And yf I shal to you playnly saye
Ouer the table / ye shal not spetel conueye — 217 or spit over it.

[32]

Yef ye be serued / with metes delicate — Share dainties with your fellows:
Departe with your felowe / in gentil wise
The clerck saith / nature is content & saciate — 220
With mene diete / and litil shall suffyse
Departe therfore / as I you deuyse
Engrose not / vnto your self alle
For gentilnes / wil aye be liberalle — 224 gentleness is liberal.

---

lene not on the table, for that rvde ys ; — [Hill's Text.]
216     & yff I shall to you playnly saye,
        over the table ye shall not spetell conveye.

¶ Yff ye be servede with metis delycate,
        Departe with your felawe in gentill wyse ;
220     the clerke seyth, 'nature ys content & sacyate
        with mene dyete, & lytill shall suffyce ;'
        Departe therfor, as I you devyce,
        Engrose not vnto yowre selfe all,
224     ffor gentylnesse will ay be lyberall.

3 *

### [33]

And wan p*er*cace youre seruice is not large,
  Grucchith not wyth frownyng countenaunce,
Ne maketh not ther-of to mekell charge,          227
  Disposeth you to goodly sufferaunce,
  And what ye haue, take hit for suffisaunce ;
    Holde you pleased wyth that god hath you sent,
    He hath Inough [1] that can hold hym content. 231    [1] MS. Inought.

### [34]

Burnysh no bonys wyth youre tethe, be ware,
  That houndis tecche fayleth of curtesie ;
But wyth youre knyff make the bonys bare ;          234
  Handell youre mete so well and so clenly,
  That ye offenden not the company
    Where ye be sette, as ferre-forth as ye can ;
    Remembre well that man*er* maketh man.          238

### [35]

And whan your teeth shall cutte youre mete small,
  Wyth open mouth be ware that ye not ete,
But loke youre lippis be closede as a wall,          241
  Whan to &[2] fro ye trauers youre mete ;          [2] MS. a.
  Kepe you so close that men haue no conceite
    To seyn of you langage of vilonye,
    Be cause ye ete youre mete vnma[ne]rly.          245

---

¶ And wha*n* percaas your s*er*vyce ys not large,          [Hill's Text.]
    Groge not wit*h* frownynge covntenavnce,
  Ne make ther of not to mykyll charge ;
228   Dyspose you to goodly suffravnce,
    & what ye haue, take yt in suffysavnce ;
      be you plesid wit*h* suche as god hath you sent ;
      he hat̄h ynowgh þat ca*n* hold hy*m* co*n*tente.

232   Burnysshe no bonys wit*h* your tet̄h, be ware,          [fl C lxlj back.]
    Suche hownd*is* tacches fallen of vncurtesye,
    but wit*h* your knyfe make the bonys bare.
      Handle your mete so well & so clenly

[33]

And whan percaas your seruise is not large

Gruccheth not / with frownyng contenaunce

Ne make therof / not to mykyl charge 227

Dispose you to goodly suffraunce

And what ye haue / take it in suffysaunce

Be ye plesid with suche as god hath you sent

He hath ynough / that can holde hym content 231

If your helping is not large, don't grumble,

but be content.

[34]

Burnysshe no bones / with your teth / beware

Suche houndis tacches / falle of vncurtesye

But with your knyf / make the bones bare 234

Handle your mete / so wel and so clenly

That ye offende not the company

Where ye be sette / as ferforth as ye can

Remembryng wel / that manners make man 238

[Leaf 6 b.] Don't burnish bones with your teeth.

Handle your food cleanly,

for Manners make Man.

[35]

Ande whan that / ye ete your mete smalle

With open mouth / beware ye not ete

But loke your lippes / be closed as a walle 241

Whan to ande fro / ye trauerse your mete

Kepe you so cloos / that men haue no conseite

To say of you / ony langage or vilonye

Bicause ye ete your mete / vnmanerly 245

Eat with your lips closed.

---

236 That ye offende not the company
wher ye be sette, as ferforthe as ye can,
Remembryng well that maners make man.

¶ And whan that ye ete your mete small,
240 with open mowth be ware ye not ete,
but loke / your lyppes be closed as a wall ;
whan to & fro ye traverse your mete,
kepe you so cloos that men haue no conceyte
244 To saye of you any langage or vylonye
by cavse ye ete your mete so vnmanerly.

[Hill's Text.]

### [36]

Be ware, my child, of laughing *ouer* mesure,
  Ye shall not Also at the borde *youre* naylis pare,
Ne pike not *youre* teth wyth *youre* knyff, I you ensure,
   Ete at *youre* messe, and odir folkes spare ;     249
    A glottou*n* can but make dissches bare,
      And of Inough he taketh neu*er* hede,
      He fedith for lust more than [1] he doth for nede.     1 MS. that.

### [37]

And whan the borde is then [as] of s*er*uice,    253
  Not replenyshide wyth gret diuercite,
Of mete and drincke good chere may than suffice,
   Hit is A signe of gret humanite,    256
    Wyth gladsom chere than fulsom for to be ;
      The poet seyth howe that the poure borde
      Men may encrese wyth cherefull wille and worde.

### [38]

And o thing, my childe, I warne you vndirstonde,
  Specially for *youre* owne honeste,
In the water wasschith so clene *youre* hande,    262
   That *youre* towell neuer ensoyled be
  .So foule that hit be lothely vnto se ;
    Wasschith wyth watire till *youre* handis be clene,
    And in *youre* clothe ther shall no spotte be sene.

---

¶ Beware, my chyld, of laughynge ou*er* mesure ;    [Hill's Text.]
   Ne at *the* borde ye sha*ll* no nayles pare,
248   Ne pyke *your* teth *with* knyf, I you ensure.
   Ete at *your* messe, & othere folk*is* spare ;
   A gloton ca*n* but make *the* bonys bare,
   & of ynowgh he takyth nevere hede,
252   he ffedyth more for lust than for nede.

¶ And wha*n* *the* borde ys thyn as of s*er*vyce,
   Nowght replenysshed *with* gret dyversit*e*
   of mete & drynke, gud chere may tha*n* suffice,
256   *with* honest talkyng ; & also owght ye

[36]

Beware my childe / of laughyng ouer mesure
Ne at the borde / ye shall no naylis pare
Ne pyke your teth / with knyf / I you ensure     248
Ete at your messe / and other folkes spare
A gloton can but make the bones bare .
Ande of ynough / he taketh neuer hede
He fedith more for lust / than for nede     . 252

*Don't pare your nails at table, or pick your teeth with a knife.*

[37]

And whan þᵉ borde is thynne / as of seruyse
Nought replenesshed with grete diuersite
Of mete & drinke good chere may theñ suffise     255
With honest talkyng / and also ought ye
With gladsom chere / thenne fulsom for to be
The poete saith / hou that a poure borde
Men may enriche / with cheerful wil & worde     259

*[Leaf 7 a.] When there are not many dishes, be satisfied with chatting cheerily.*

[38]

And one thyng my chylde / ye vnderstonde     .
In especyalle / for your owne honeste
In the water / wasshe so clene your honde     262
That your towel / neuer enfoyled be
So fowle / that it be lothsom on to see
Wasshe with water / your hondes so cleene
That in the towel shal no spotte be sene     266

*Wash your hands clean in the water, so as to leave no dirt on your towel.*

---

       with gladsum chere then fulsome for to be :     [Hill's Text.]
       The poete seyth how that ' a powre borde
259     Men may enryche with cherfull will & worde.'

¶ And on thyng, my child, ye vnderstond,
      In especyall for your own honeste :
      In the water wasshe so clene your hond
      that your towell never ensoyled be
264     So fowle that yt be lothsome on to see ;
      wasshe with water your hondis so clene
      that in the towell shall no spote be sene.

[39]

L eue not youre spone in youre dissche standyng,
　Ne vppon the brede hit shall not lie ;
Lette youre trenchoure be clene for eny thyng,　　269
　Yif ye haue no chaunge, yit as honestly
　As ye can, maketh avoydie,
　　So that no fragment from youre trenchoure falle ;
　　Do this, my childe, in chambre and in halle.　273

[40]

W han Another spekoth at the table,
　Be ware ye interrupte¹ not is tale nor langage,
For that is a thing discommendable,　　276
　And hit is no signe of folkes sage
　To ben of wordis besy and outrage ;
　　For the wyse man seyth pleinly in sentence,
　　'He shall be wyse that yevith Audience.'　280

¹ MS. *corruptly has* nattiripte.

[41]

V ndre-stondeth ther-fore or than ye speke,
　Printyng in youre mynde clerely the sentence,
He that vseth A mannes tale to breke　　283
　Lettyth vncurtesly the Audience,
　And hurtyth hym-sylf for lacke of silence ;
　　He may not yeue answere convenyent
　　That herith not fynally what is ment.　287

¶ lete not your spone in youre disshe stond,
268　Ne vpon the table yt shuld not lye ;
　lete your trenchowre be clene for any thyng,
　& yf ye haue, change yet as honestly
　As ye can ; make avoyde manerly
272　So that no fragment fro your trenchere fall :
　Do thus, my child, in chambere & in hall.

¶ And whan a-nother man spekyth at the table,
　be ware ye interrupte not his langage,
276　for that ys a thyng on-comendable,
　& yt ys not no signe of folkis sage

*[Hill's Text.]*

## [39]

Lete not your spone / in your disshe‧stonding
Ne vpon the table / it shold not lye
Lete your trenchour / be clene for ony thing    269
And yf ye haue chañge / yet as honestly
As ye can / make a voyde manerly
So that no fragment / fro your trencher falle
Do thus my childe / in chambre & in halle    273

*Don't leave your spoon in your dish or on the table.*
*Keep your trencher clean.*

## [40]

And whan another man / spekith atte table
Beware ye enterrupte not / his langage
For that is a thinge discomendable    276
Ande it is no signe of folkes sage
To be of langage / besy ande outrage
For the wyse man saide / in his sentence
He sholde be wyse / that gyueth audience    280

*[Leaf 7 b.]*
*Don't interrupt man in his talk.*

## [41]

Vnderstonde therfore or than ye speke
Prynte in your mynde / clerly the sentence
Who that vsith / a mannes tale to breke    283
Letteth vncurteysly / alle the audyence
Ande hurteth hym self / for lack of science
He may not gyue answere conuenyente
That herith not fynally / what is mente    287

*Before you speak, settle in your mind what you have to say.*

---

To be of langage besy & owtrage ;
ffor the wyse sayd in his sentence
280    'he shuld be hold [& be wyse]¹ *that* gevyth
audyence.'

*[Hill's Text.]*
*[1 In a later hand, above the line.]*

¶ Vnderstond *ther*for or than ye speke ;
prynt *in* your mynde clerly *the* sentence ;
who *that* vsyth a ma*n*ys tale to breke,
284    lettyth v̇ncurteysly aȴ the audyence
And hurteth hy*m* self for lake of scyence ;
he maye not geve answere co*n*venyente
*that* heryth not‧fynally what ys mente.

*[fl C lxiij.]*

[42]

Be ware Also, my childe, of rehersaille
 Of materis whiche ben at the table mevide ;
Hit grevith ofte and dothe men disavaylle,        290
 Full many a man that vice hath mysschevide,
 Of evill thyng saide is wors often contrivide ;
  Suche reportis alway loke ye esschewe,
  As may of olde frendis make enemyes newe.   294

[43]

A vise you well whan ye take youre disporte,
 Honest games that ye haunte and vse,
And suche as ben of violente reporte,        297
 I counsell you, my childe, that ye refuse ;
 For trustith well ye shall nout you excuse
  From berchely fest, yef I may you aspie
  Playng at ¹ eny game of rebaudie.        301        ¹ MS. or.

[44]

Itt is to A goodly childe well syttyng,
 To vse disportis of myrth and plesaunce,
To harpe and lute, or lustely to syng,        304
 And in the pres ryght manerly to daunce ;
 When men se A childe of suche gouernaunce,
  They seyn, ' gladde may this [childes] frendis be
  To haue a sone soo manerly as he.'        308

---

¶ But beware, my child, also of rehersayle        [*Hill's Text.*]
289  Off maters whiche be at the table meved ;
    It greweth ¹ ofte, & doth men dysavayle ;        [¹ The line is over the *th*.]
    ffull many a man that vyce hathe myscheved ;
292  Off evyll thynke sayd, ys worse contryved ;
    Suche reportes alwaye, my child, eschewe,
    As may of olde frendis make enmyes newe.

¶ Avyse you well whan ye take your dysporte,
296  honeste games that ye hawnt & vse ;
    & suche as bene of vyleyns report,
    I cownsell you, my child, that ye refuse ;

### [42]

But beware my childe / also of rehersaylle  
Of maters / whiche ben atte table meuide  
It greuith ofte / ande doth men disauayle     290  
Ful many a man / þᵗ vice hath myscheuide  
Of euyl thinge saide / is werse contryuide  
Suche reportis / alway my childe eschewe  
As may of olde frendis / make enemyes newe     294

*Don't repeat what you hear at table,*

### [43]

Aduise you wel whan ye take your disporte  
Honest games / that ye haunte ande vse  
And suche as ben of vylayns reporte     297  
I counceyl you my chyld / that ye refuse  
For truste ye wel / ye shal you not excuse  
From brecheles feste / and I may you espye  
Playnge at ony game of Rybawdrye     301

*[Leaf 8 a.] Play only at proper games.*

### [44]

It is to a godly chyld wel syttynge  
To vse disportes of myrthe & plesañce  
To harpe or lute / or lustely to synge     304  
Or in the prees right manerly to daunce  
Whan men se a chyld of suche gouernance  
They saye / glad may this chyldis frendis be  
To haue a chylde / so manerly as is he     308

*You should, harp, lute, sing, or dance.*

---

<table>
<tr><td></td><td>ffor truste ye well ye shall you not excuse</td><td>[Hill's Text.]</td></tr>
<tr><td>300</td><td>ffrom brecheles feste, & I may you espye</td><td></td></tr>
<tr><td></td><td>Playenge at any game of rebawdrye.</td><td></td></tr>
</table>

¶ Ytt ys to a goodly child well syttyng  
    To vse dysportes of myrth & plesavnce,  
304  to harpe, to lute, or lustyly to synge,  
    Or in the prees right manerly to davnce.  
    whan men se a child of suche governavnce,  
    thei saye, ' glade may this childis frendys be  
308  To haue a child so manerly as ys he.'

[45]

Exersice youre-selfe also in redyng
     Of bokys enournede wyth eloquence ;
Ther shall ye fynde both plesaunce and lernyng,        311
     And so ye may in euery good presence
     Some [what] fynde and see as in sentence,
          That shall accorde the tyme to ocupie,
          That ye not nede to stondyn idelie.        315

[46]

Itt¹ is fare to be cominycatyfe        ¹ MS. IIt.
     In matires vnto purpoos according,
So that a wight sume not excessyfe,        318
     For trusteth well, hit is tedious thyng
     For to here a childe multiplie talkyng,
          Yif hit be not to the purpose applied,
          And also wyth goodly termys aleyde.        322

[47]

Redith Gower in his writyng moralle,
     That auñcient faders memorie,
Redith his bokis clepide 'confessionalle,'        325
     Wyth many anodir vertuous tretie,
     Full of sentence sette so frutuously,
          That them to rede shall yeue you corage,
          So is he fulle of sentence and langage.        329

---

¶ Excersyse also your selfe in redyng        [Hill's Text.]
     Off bokes enorned with eloquence,
     ther shall ye fynde both plesyre & lernynge,
312  so that ye may in euery good presence
     Some-what fynde as in sentence
          that shall accorde the tyme to occupye,
          That ye not nede to stonde ydellye.

¶ It ys fayer to be comynycatyfe
317     In maters vnto purpose accordyng,
     So that a wyghte seme exersyfe ;
     ffor trustyth well yt ys a tedyovs thyng

### [45]

Excersise your self also in redynge

Of bookes enornede with eloquence

Ther shal ye fynde / bothe plesir & lernynge 311

So thaþ ye may / in euery good presence

Somwhat fynde / as in sentence

That shal acorde / the tyme to ocupy

That ye not nede / to stonden ydelly 315

Practise reading of eloquent books.

### [46]

It is fayr / for to be comynycatyf

In maters vnto purpose acordynge

So that a wyght seme excersyf 318

For trusteth wel / it is a tedyous thynge

For to here a chylde / multeplye talkyng

Yf it be not to the purpose applyede

Ande also with / goodly termys alyede 322

[Leaf 8 b.]
It is right to talk pertinently,

but a bore if the talk is irrelevant.

### [47]

Redeth gower in his wrytynge moralle

That auncyent [1] fader of memorye

Redeth his bookes / callede confessionalle 325

With many another vertuous trayttye

Ful of sentence / set ful fructuosly

That hym to rede / shal gyue you corage

He is so ful of fruyt. sentence and langage 329

Read Gower's

1 Orig. anucyent.

*Confessio Amentis,*

---

320 ffor to here a child multyply talkyng

    yf yt be not to *the* purpose applyed,

    & also w*ith* goodly termes alyed.

¶ Redyth gover *in* his wrytyng moraℏ,

324    That Auncyente ffader of memorye,

    Redyth his bookes called c*on*fessyonaℏ,

    w*ith* many a-nothere vertuvs tretye

    ffuℏ of sentence sett fuℏ fructvously,

328    That hy*m* to rede shaℏ geve you covrage,

    he ys so fuℏ of frute, se*n*tence, & langage.

[*Hill's Text.*]

### [48]

O Fader and Founder of eternate eloquence,
  That eluminede all this oure britaigne ;
To sone we lost his lauriate presence,    332
  O lusty licoure of that fulsome fountaigne ;
  Cursed deth, why hast thou this poete slayne,
    I mene Fadir chaucers, mastir Galfride ?
    Allas ! the while, that euer he from vs diede.  336

### [49]

Redith his bokys fulle of all plesaunce,
  Clere in sentence, in longage excellent,
Brefly to wryte suche was his suffesaunce,    339
  What-euer to sey he toke in his entent,
  His longage was so feyre and pertinent,
    That semed vnto mennys heryng,
    Not[1] only the worde, but verrely the thing.  343    1 MS. But.

### [50]

Redith, my child, redith his warkys all,
  Refuseth non, they ben expedient ;
Sentence or langage, or both, fynde ye shall    346
  Full delectable, for that fader ment
  Of all his purpos and his hole entent
    Howe to plese in euery audience,
    And in oure toung was well of eloquence.  350

---

  ¶ O fader & fownder of ornate eloquence    [Hill's Text.]
    that Illumyned hast all owre bretayne !    [ffl O lxiij back.]
332  To sone we loste thy lavreat science,
    O lusty lyqvovre of that fulsum fontayne !
    O cursed deth ! why hast thou that poete slayne,
    I mene fader chavucer, mayster galfryde ?
336    Alas the while that ever he from vs dyed !

  ¶ Redyth his werkes full of plesavnce,
    Clere in sentence, In langage excellente :
    Bryefly to wryte, such was his suffysavnce,
340  What-evere to say he toke in his entente,

### [48]

O fader and founder of ornate eloquence

That enlumened hast alle our bretayne

To soone we loste / thy laureate scyence     332

O lusty lyquour / of that fulsom fontayne

O cursid deth / why hast thou þᵗ poete slayne

I mene fader chaucer / maister galfryde

Alas the whyle / that euer he from vs dyde     336

and the Father
and Founder of
Eloquence,

[Leaf 163, back.]

mayster Galfryde
Chawcer,

### [49]

Redith his werkis / ful of plesaunce

Clere in sentence / in langage excellent

Briefly to wryte / suche was his suffysance     339

What euer to saye / he toke in his entente

His langage was so fayr and pertynente

It semeth vnto mannys heerynge

Not only the worde / but verely the thynge     343

[Leaf 9 a.]
whose works are
full of pleasaunce,

whose language

seems not only
words, but truly
things.

### [50]

Redeth my chylde / redeth his bookes alle

Refuseth none / they ben expedyente

Sentence or langage / or bothe fynde ye shalle     346

Ful delectable / for that good fader mente

Of al his purpose / and his hole entente

How to plese in euery audyence

And in our tunge / was welle of eloquence     350

Read all his
books; refuse
none :

he is delightful.

---

his langage was so fayere & pertynente,

     yt semeth vnto manys heryng

343     Not only the worde, but veryly the thyng.

¶ Redyth, my child, redyth his bookes all,

     Refusith Non, they ben expedyente ;

     sentence or langage, both fynd ye shall ;

     ffull delectable that good fader mente,

348     for all his purpose & his hole entente

     [was] how to please in euery audyence,

     & In owre tonge was well of Eloquence.

[Hill's Text.]

[51]

Beholde Oclyff in his translacion,
In goodly langage and sentence passing wyse,
Yevyng the prince suche exortacion     353
   As to his highnesse he coude best devyse.
    Of trouth, peace, of mercy, and of Iustice,
     And odir vertuys, sparing for no slouthe
     To don his devere, and quiten hym, as trouth 357

[52]

Required hym, anenste his souereyne,
Most dradde and louyd, whos excellent highnesse
He aduertysede by his writing playne,     360
   To vertue perteynyng to the nobles
   Of a prince, and berith wyttenesse
    His trety entitlede ' of regyment,'
    Compyled of most entier true entent.     364

[53]

Loketh Also vppon dan Iohn lidgate,
My mastire, whilome clepid monke of bury,
Worthy to be renownede laureate,     367
   I pray to gode, in blis his soule be mery,
   Synging ' Rex Splendens,' the heuenly ' kery,'
    Among the muses ix celestiall,
    Afore the hieghest Iubiter of all.     371

---

¶ Behold Ocklyf in his transslacion,[1]     [Hill's Text.]
352    In goodly langage & sentence passyng wyse     [1 transflacion]
   howe he gewyth his prince such exortacion
   As to the hyeste he covld best devyse
   Off trowth / pees / mercy / & Iustyse,
356    & vertu, lettyng for no slowth
   To do his devoyre & qvyte hym his trowth.

¶ Requyre hym As Agaynst his soverayne,
   moste Drade & loved, whose excellent hyenes
360    he advertysed by his wrytyng playne
   To vertu aperteynyng to nobles

[51]

Beholde Ocklyf in his translac*i*on

In goodly langage / & sente*n*ce passyng wyse

How he gyueth his prynce / suche exortac*i*on     353

As to the hyest / he coude best deuyse

Of trouthe. pees. mercy. and Iustise

And vertues / leetyng for no slouthe

To do his deuoir & quite him of his trouthe     357

*Read Occlevetoo,*
*who gave his Prince such wise advice*

[52]

Require*de* hym / as ayenst his souerayne

Most drad*e* & louyd*e* / wos excellent hyeues

He aduertysed*e* / by his wrytyng*e* playne     360

To vertu / apperteynyng to nobles

Of a prynce / as bereth good*e* witnes

His traytye / entitled*e* of regymente

Compyled*e* of entyer trewe entente     364

*[Leaf 9 b.]*

*in his treatise De Regimine Principum.*

[53]

Loke also / vpon dan Io*h*n lydgate

My maister whylome / monke of berye

Worthy to be renomed*e* / as poete laureate     367

I praye to god*e* in blysse his soule be mercy

Syngyng*e* Rex splendens that heuenly kyrye

Amonge the muses nyne celestyall*e*

Byfore the hyest Iubyter of all*e*     371

*John Lydgate, too, my master.*

*(I pray God his soul is singing Rex splendens*

---

Off a *pri*nce, as beryth god wytnes,

     hys treatye entytled of regemente,

364     Compyled of entyer trewe entente.

¶ Loke also than vpon Iohan lydgate,

     My mayrster, whylom monke of bury,

     worthy to be renomed As poete lavreate ;

368     I p*r*ay to god in blysse his sowle be mery,

     Syngyng / Rex splendens / *that* hevenly Kyrye,

     Amonge *the* mvses nyne celestyatt

     be-fore *th*e hyghest Iubyter of att,

*[Hill's Text.]*

4

[54]

I not why deth my mastire dide envie,
But for he shulde chaunge his habite ;
Pety hit is that suche a man shulde die !     374
  But nowe I trist he be a carmylite ;
  His amyse blacke is chaunged into white,
    Among the muses ix celestiall,
    Afore the hieghest Iubiter of all ;     378

[55]

Passing the muses all of elicone,
Where is ynympariable of Armonye,
Thedir I trist my mastir-is soule is gone,     381
  The sterrede palays aboue dapplede skye,
  Ther to syng ' sanctus ' incessantly
    Among the muses ix celestiall,
    Affore the highest Iubiter of all.     385

[56]

Redith is volumes that ben so large and wyde,
Souereynly sitte in sadnesse of sentence,
Elumynede wyth colouris fresshe on euery syde,     388
 Hit passith my wytte, I haue no eloquence
  To yeue hym lawde aftir his excellence,
    For I dare say he lefte hym not on lyue,
    That coude his cunnyng suffisantly discreue.    392

---

372     [Omitted.  See Preface, p. ii.]     [Hill's Text.]


376


  ¶ Passyng the mvses nyne of elycon,
380    Wher ys no pareyll of Armonye ;
    Thyder I trust my Maysters sowle be gon,
     The sterred paleys above the dappled skye,

[54]

[Omitted.    See Preface, p. ii.]

374


378

[55]

Passynge the muses nyne of Elycon
Where is non pareyl of armonye
Thider I truste my meistres soule begone          381   in the starred
The sterride paleys / aboue the dapplyd skye          palace above the
    dappled sky,
There to synge sanctus incessantly                    before the
Amonge the muses ix celestyalle
Byfore the hyest / Iubiter of alle                385   highest
    Jupiter of all.)

[56]

Redeth his volumes / that ben large & wyde            [Leaf 10 a.]
    Read his large
Seueryly set / in sadnes of sentence                  volumes
Enlumyned with colours fressh on euery side       388
Me lacketh witte / I haue none eloquence            illuminated with
  fresh colours.
To gyue hym lawde / after his excellence
For I dar saye / he lefte hym not a lyue
That coude his connyng / sufficiently discriue    392

---

    Ther to syng sanctus insessavntly          *Hill's Text.*]
384    Emonge the mvses nyne celestyall,
    Before *the* hyeste Iubyter of all.

  ¶ Redyth hys volumes *that* be large & wyde,
    Severyly sette in sadnes of sentence,
388  Enlumined *with* colovres fresshe on eu*er*y side.   [ffi C lxiiij.]
    Me lakketh wytt, I haue non eloquence,
    To geve hy*m* lawde after his excellence,
    ffor I dare saye he lefte hy*m* not alyve
392    That covde his cu*n*yng ssufficiently discryve.
    4 *

### [57]

But his werkys his laude moste nede conquere,
He may neuer oute of remembrance die,
His werkys shall his [name ¹] conuey and bere     395   ¹ MS. *here repeats* werkys.
    Aboute the world all-most eternallie ;
    Lette his owne werkys prayse hym and magnifie ;
       I dare not preyse, for fere that I offende,
       My lewde langage shuld rather appeyre than amend.

### [58]

Lo, my childe, thes good faders Auñcient
Repide the feldis fresshe of fulsumnesse,
The floures feyre they gadderid vp and hent,     402
    Of siluereus langage the tresoure and richesse ;
    Who wolle hit haue, my litle childe, doutelesse
       Must of hem begge, ther is no more to say,
       For of oure toung they were bothe locke and key.

### [59]

There can no man there fames nowe disteyne,
Thanbawmede toung and aureate sentence,
Men gette hit nowe by cantelmele, and gleyne     409
    Here and there wyth besy diligence,
    And fayne wolde riche the crafte of eloquence ;
       But be the glaynes is hit often sene,
       In whois feldis they glayned haue and bene.     413

---

¶ But his werkes his lavde must nede conquere ;     [*Hill's Text.*]
    *the*i may never owt of remembravnce dye ;
    hys werkes shaʈ his name conveye & bere
396     Abowte *the* world almoste eternelly.
    lete his owne werk*is* prayse lym, & magnyfye;
    I dare not prayse, leest for fere I offende;
    My langage shuld rathere apayere tha*n* amend.

¶ Loo, my child, this faders avncyente
401     Repen *the* fyldes ffresshe of fulsomnes ;
    *the* flowres fresshe thei gadered vp, & hente.
    Off syluer langage *the* greate ryches

[57]

But his werkis / his laude / must nede conquere His works
.They may neuer / out of remembraunce dye
His werkis shal his name conueye & bere 395 shall bear his
Aboute the worlde / almost eternely name about the
world almost
Lete his owen werkis preyse hym & magnefie eternally.
I dar not preyse / for fere lest I offende
My langage / shold rather apeyre than amende 399

[58]

Loo my childe / these faders auncyente [Leaf 10 b.]
These ancient
Repen the feldes fresshe of fulsomnes fathers reaped the
fields,
The flours fresh they gadred vp & hente 402 and gathered the
flowers.
Of siluer langage / the grete riches He who wants
silver words
Who wil it haue my lityl childe doutles must beg of them.
Muste of hem begge / ther is no more to saye
For of our tunge / they were both lok & kaye 406

[59]

Ther can noman now her werkis disteyne
The enbamed tunge / and aureate sentence
Men gete it now / by cantelmele & gleyne 409 Now we only
glean,
Here and there by besy diligence
And fayne wold reche / her craft of eloquence and by the
gleaning one sees
And by the gleyne / it is ful oft sene in whose fields the
In whos felde / the gleyners haue bene 413 gleaners have
been.

---

404 who will yt haue, my child, dowtles [Hill's Text.]
Muste of them bege: there ys no more to saye,
ffor of owre tonge thei were both loke & keye ;

¶ Ther can no man ther werkes dysteyne :
408 The enbamed tonge & avreat sentence,
Men gete yt now by cantelmele, & glene
here & there by besy delygence,
& fayne wold reche ther crafte of eloqvence ;
412 & by the gleyne ytt ys full ofte sene
In whose fylde the gleners haue bene.

## [60]

As vnto me Age hath bede good morowe,
　I am not able clenly for to gleyne,
Nature is feyne of crafte here eien to borowe,　　416
　Me fayleth clerenesse of myn eien tweyne ;
　Begge I may, I can no gleyn certeyn,
　　Ther-for that werke I wolle playnly remytte
　　To folke yong, more persaunt clere of wytte.　420

## [61]

And syke also, and in case ye fynde
　Suche gleynes fresch as hath some apparence
Of fayre langage, yet take them and vnbynde,　　423
　And preueth what they beth in existence,
　Coloured in langage, savory in sentence,
　　And dou[te]th not, my childe, wythoute drede,
　　Hit woll profite such thyng to se and rede.　427

## [62]

Yit eft-sonnys, my childe, let vs resorte
　To the intente of oure fyrst matiere
Digresside, somwhat fulle we wolld reporte,　　430
　And reuyue the lawde of them that were
　Founders of oure langage, thilke fadyrs dere,
　　Who-is soulis god [aboue] in b[l]esse inhaunce
　　That lusten so oure langage to Avaunce.　434

---

¶ And vnto my age bot good morowe　　　*[Harl. Text.]*
　I am not able clerly for to gleyne,
416　Nature ys fayne of crafte her eyen to borow ;
　Me lakketh clernes of myne eyen twayne ;
　Begge I may / gleyne I may not certeyne ;
　*ther*fore *that* werke I will playnly remytte
420　To folk*is* yong, more passyng clere of wyte.

¶ Seche ye *ther*fore, & in caas ye fynde
　suche glenars fresshe as haue sum apparens
　Off fayer la*n*gage, yet take them, & vnbynde,
424　& preve ye what *thei* be i*n* existence

[60]

And vnto me / age hath bode good morowe
I am not able clenly / for to gleyne — I cannot glean,
Nature is fayn of craft / her eyen to borowe      416
Me lacketh clerenes / of myn eyen tweyne
Begge I maye / gleyne I can not certeyne — I can only beg:
Therfore þᵗ werck / I wil playnly remytte — gleaning I give
To folkis yong / more passyng clere of witte   420 up to younger folks.

[61]

Seche ye therfore / and in caas ye fynde — If you find such gleaners,
Such gleynors fressh as haue som apparence
Of fayr langage / yet take hem & vnbynde   423 unbind their sheaves:
And preue ye / what they be in existence
Colourd in langage / sauerly in sentence — their fair speech
And doubte not my childe / withoute drede
It wil prouffite to see suche thingis & red[e] ¹  427 will profit you.

[62]

Yet eft sones my childe / lete vs resorte — [Leaf 11 a.] But let us return to our first subject.
To thentente of yur first matere
Degressed somwhat / for we wold reporte   430
And reuiue the laude of hem that were
Famous in our langage / these faders dere
Whos sowles in blysse / god eternel auaunce
That lysten so our langage to enhaunce      434

¹ A hole in the paper.

[Hill's Text.]

Colovred in langage, saverly in sentence,
& dowte not, my child, with-owt drede
427    yt will profet to se such thyngis, & rede.

¶ Ye, efte-soones, my child, let vs resorte
To the yntent of your fyrst matere
Degressed somwhat, for we wolde reporte
& revyue the lawde of them that were
432    famovs in owre langage, thise faders dere
whos ¹ sowles in blis, god eternall avaunce,
that lysten sone owre langage to enhavnce !

¹ The s is by a later hand.

[63]

Than, litle childe, I councelle you that ye
 Take hede vnto the norture that men vse,
Newe founden or Auncient whet[h]er hit be,     437
 So shall no man youre curteyse refuse ;
 The guise and custome shall you, my childe, excuse ;
 Mennys werkys haue often entirchaunge,
 That nowe is norture, sumtyme had ben full straunge.

[64]

Thinges whilome vside ben layde aside,
 And new fetis dayly ben contryvyde,
Men[nys actes] can in no plight abyde,     444
 They ben chaungeable and oft mevide,
 Thing some-tyme alowide is nowe reprevide,.
 And aftir this shall thingis vppe aryse,
 That men sette nowe but [at] litle a prise.     448

[65]

Thus mene I, my childe, that ye shull vse and haunte
 The guise of them that don most manerly,
But be ware of vnthrefte ruskyn galaunte,     451
 Counterfetoure vncunnyng of curtesie,
 His tecches ben infecte wyth vilonye,
 Vngerde, vnblesside, seruyng at the table,
 Me semeth hym seruaunt full pendable.    455

---

¶ Then litill Iohñ, I consayle you that ye     [Hill's Text.]
436    Take hede to the nortvres that men vse,    [fl C lxiiij back.]
 newe fownd or avncyent, whether yt be ;
 So shall no man your curtesye refuse ;
 the gyse & custum, my child, shall you excuse.
440    Menys werkes haue oftyn enterchavnce ;
 that nowys norture, somtyme hath be stravnge;

¶ Thyngis whylom vsed be now layd a-syde,
 & newe fetes dayly be contryved :
444   Menys actes can in no plyte abyde,
 They be chavngable & ofte meved ;

## [63]

Thenne lityl Iohn / I counceyl you that ye

Take hede to the norture / that men vse

Newe founde / or auncyent whether it be            437

So shal no man / your curtoisye refuse

The guyse & custom / my child shal you excuse

Mennys werkis / haue often enterchange

That nowe is norture / somtyme had be strañge      441

*Little Jack,*

*take heed to the manners of your time,*

*for customs change,*

## [64]

Thingis whilom vsed / ben now leyd a syde

And newe feetis / dayly ben contreuide

Mennys actes / can in no plyte abyde             444

They be changeable ande ofte meuide

Thingis somtyme alowed / is now repreuid

And after this / shal thinges vp aryse

That men set now / but at lytyl pryse            448

*new ways are invented every day,*

*and will be hereafter.*

## [65]

This mene I my childe / þᵗ ye shal haunte

The guyse of them / that do most manerly

But beware of vnthryft Ruskyn galañte            451

Counterfeter of vnconnyng curtoisye

His tacchis ben enfecte with vilonye

Vngyrte. vnblyssed. seruyng atte table

Me semeth hym a seruañt nothing able             455

*[Leaf 11 b.] Imitate the well-mannered, and beware of ruskyn gallants*

*of bad habits,*

*serving ungirt,*

---

thynges sumtyme alowed be now repreved ;

& after this shall thynges vp a-ryse

448    that men sett now but at lytill pryse :

¶ This mene I, my child, *that* ye shall havnte

*the* gyse of the*m that* do most manerly ;

but be ware of onthryft¹ ruskyn gallavnte,

452    Conterfetter² of vnconnyng curtessy,

hys taches ben enfecte *with* vylonye ;

Vngerte / vnblessed / *ser*vyng at table,

Me semeth hy*m* a *ser*vavnte no thyng able ;

*[Hill's Text.]*

*1 A later hand has added y.*

*2 The r is by a later hand.*

### [66]

Wynter ne somer to his souerayne
    Chappron hardy no bonet lust avale,
For euery worde yeuyng his maister tweyne,        458
    Vaunparlere in euery mannes tale,
    Absolon wyth the disculede heres smalle ;
    ·Lyke to A presener of seint Malouse,
    A sonny bush myght cause hym to goo louse. 462

### [67]

O I passe norture ! fy ! fy ! for schame !
    I shuld haue seide he myght go hauke and hunt,
For that schuld be A gentilmannys game,        465
    To suche disportis thes gentis folkys be wounte ;
    I seide to ferre, my langage was to blounte,
    But of this galaunte, loo ! loke a while & fele,
    He feccheth his compace whan he shall bowe or knele,

### [68]

Braced so straytly th[at h]e ¹ may not plie,        ¹ MS. the.
    But gaderith hit in by maner of wyndlese,
And ȝif he wrenche aside or lytil wrye,        472
    His gere stonte all in pertous ² case,        ² *Read* perlous ?
    The scho, the hose, the point, doublet, and lace ;
    And if ought breke, somme thinges ³ that ben badde        ³ *Read* tounges.
    Shall sey anon, ' a knaue hath broke a ladde.' 476

---

    ¶ Wynter & somer to his soverayne        [Hill's Text.]
457        Capron hardy, no bonet lyst to avaylé,
        For euery worde geveyng his mayster twayne,
        avavntparler In euery manys tale,
460        Absolon with disheveld heres smale,
        lyke to a prysoner of saynt malowes,
        A sonny busshe able to the galowes.

    ¶ O ! I passe nortvre ! fy, fy, for sham !
464        I myght haue said he shuld go havke & honte,
        ffor that shuld be a gentylman[i]s game,
        To suche dysportis gentiƚƚ folkis be wonte ;

## [66]

Wynter and somer to his souereyne

Capron hardy / no bonet lyste to auale

For euery word / gyui*n*g his maister tweyne 458

Auauntparler / in euery mannys tale

Absolon with disheueld heeris smale

Lyke to a prysoner of seynt malowis

A sonny busshe / able to go to the galowis 462

*not doffing his cap to his master,*

*forward in speech, rough-haired,*

*and lousy-headed,*

## [67]

O I passe norture fy fy for shame

I myght haue said he shold go hauke & honte

For that shold be a gentilmans game 465

To such disportes / gentil folkes be wonte

I sayd to ferre / my langage was to blonte

But yet sir galante wha*n* ye shal bowe or knele

He goth by compace round as doth a whele 469

*(though it's hardly good manners to say so.)*

*When he tries to kneel, he works round like a wheel,*

## [68]

Braced so strayt / that he may not plye

But gaderith it / by maner of a wyndelas

And he ought wrenche a syde / or a litil wrie . 472

His geer stondeth then*n*e / in ful parlo*us* caas

His sho / his hose / doblet / point & laas

And yf ought breke / som*m*e tu*n*ges þᵗ be bad*e*

Wil mocke & saie / a knaue hath broke a lad 476

*[Leaf 12 a.] being braced so tight that he can't bend. If he twists, a lace is like to crack.*

---

[*Hrl's Text.*]

468   1 sayd to ferre, my langage was but blonte ;
     but yet, sir gallavnt, wha*n* ye shal̃ bowe or
        knele
     he goth by *com*passe rovnd as doth a whele.

¶ Brased so streyte þat he may not plye,
     but gaderyth yt by manere of a wyndlas ;
472   & he awght wrench a-side, or a litil̃ wrye,
     hys gere stondyth the*m* *in* ful̃ *par*lovs caas,
     hys sho // his hose / doblet, poynt & laas ;
        & yff owght breke, sum tonges *that* be bade
476   wil̃ moke & say, "A knave hath broke a
        lade."

### [69]

Lat galaunte go, I mene, recheles ruskyn ;
Take hede, my childe, to suche as ben cunnyng,
So shall ye wyrship best conquere and wynne,      479
Enforsith you in all youre demenyng
To sewe vertu, and[1] from foly declynyng ;      *1 Omit and.*
And, my childe, that ye loue of honeste,
Which is accordyng wyth humanyte.      483

### [70]

That is, to you to vndirstond And knowe,
That youre aray be manerly and resonable,
Not appeissh knawen[2] and to mowe,      486      *2 Sic.*
I[n] nyse aray that is not couenable,
Fetis founde be folkys vnprofitable,
That maketh this worlde so pleynly transformate,
That men semen almost effeminate.      490

### [71]

Pley not Iakke mAlaperte, that is to sey,
Be ware of presumpcioun, be ware of pride,
Take not the fyrst place, my childe, be no way,      493
Till odir be sette manerly abyde,
Presomcion is often sette asyde,
And Avalith f[r]om his highe[3] de-gre,      *3 MS. hight.*
And he sette vppe that hath humanite.      497

---

¶ Lete gallant go ! I mene, recheles ruskyn :      *[Hill's Text.]*
Take hede my child to suche as be connyng,
so shall ye best worship conqvere & wynne ;
480      Enforce you in all your demenyng
To folowe vertu, & fro foly declynnyng ;
& weyte well that ye love honeste
which ys accordyng vnto humanyte.

¶ That ys for you to vnderstond & knowe,
485      that your araye be manerly resonable,
Not apysshe vnto moke ne to mowe ;
To nyce araye that ys not commendable,      *[Ihū 1508 per Richard hill ‖ ffl C lxv]*

### [69]

Lete galante go / I mene recheles ruskyñ

Take hede my chyld to suche as be connyng

So shal ye best worship conquere & wynne 479

Enforce you in al your demenynge

To folowe vertu / & fro folye declynynge

And waite wel that ye loue honeste

Whiche is acordynge [1] vnto humanyte 483

### [70]

That is for you / to vnderstonde & knowe

That your araye / be manerly resonable

Not apysshe / on to mocken ne to mowe 486

To nyce araye / that is not commendable

Fetis newe founden [2] by foolis vnprouffitable

That make þe world so plainly transformate

That men semen almoste enfemynate 490

### [71]

Playe not Iack malapert / that is to saye

Beware of presumpcion / beware of pryde [3]

Take not þe first place my child by the waye 493

Tyl other be sette / right manerly abyde

Presumptuous ben often set a syde.

Ande alleday aualyde / as men may see

And he is sette vp / that hath humylyte 497

[1] *Orig.* acordynge.  [2] *Orig.* fonuden.  [3] *Orig.* pryte.

---

488  ffetys, newe fonden by foolis vnprofytable,
  *that* make *the* worlde so playnly transformate
  *that* me*n* seme*n* Almost enfemynate.

 ¶ Playe not Iacke maleperte, *that* ys to say,
492 be ware of presumpc*i*on, be ware of pryde ;
  take not *the* first place, my child, by *the* waye ;
  till oder be sette, ryght manerly a-byde,
  presumtvous be ofte sette a-syde
496 & all day avaled, as me*n* may see,
  & he ys sette vp *that* hath humylyte.

[72]

T̲o̲ [1] cunnyng persones regarde ye take,          1 MS. The.
Where ye be sette in right atentif wyse,
Connyng folke cunnyng folke shulde make,          500
To theire goodnesse ye shalle make youre summise,
And as thei do, ye mosten deuyse ;
For this, my childe, is as the gospell treue,
Whoo wolle be cunnyng muste the cunnyng sewe.

[73]

A̲nd o thing I charge you speciall[ie],
To womanhode good kepe you take alway,
And them to serue loke that ye haue an eie,          507
Ther comaundementis, my childe, loke ye obey,
Plesaunt wordis to them I warne you saye,
And in all wyse do youre dilligence,
To do them plesure, honoure, and reuerence.          511

[74]

A̲s at this tyme this tretice shall suffice,
Disposeth you to kepe in youre mynde
The doctrines whiche for you I deuyse,          514
And douteth not, fulle welle ye shall hit fynde ;
To youre honoure enrolle hit vp and bynde
Ryght in youre brest, and in youre ryper age
I shall wryten you here-of the surplusage.          518

---

¶ To connyng persones regarde ye take,          [Hill's Text.]
wher ye be sette, right in ententyf wyse ;
500    Connyng folke connyng men shall make ;
to ther connyng ye shall make your surmyse,
& as thei do, ye must your selfe devyse ;
ffor this, my child, ys as the gospell trewe,
504    'who will be connyng, he must connyng sewe.'

¶ And on thyng I warne you specyally :
to womanhede take awe alway,
& them to serve loke ye haue an eye,
508    & ther comavndmentis that ye obeye ;

### [72]

To connynde persoñs regarde ye take

Where ye be sette / right in ententyf wyse

Connyng folk / connyng men shal make          500

To their connyng ye shal make your surmise

And as they do / ye muste your self deuyse

For this my childe / is as the gospel trewe

Who wil be connyng / he must þᵉ connyng sewe     504

Watch knowing
folk, and

their skill.

### [73]

And one thing / I warne you specyally

To womanhede / take awe alweye

And them to serue / loke ye haue an eye          507

And theire commandementis that ye obeye

Plesant wordes I auyse you to them seye

And in alle wyse / do ye your diligence

To do them plesure / and reuerence              511

Specially attend
to women, and

speak pleasant
words to them.

### [74]

And at this tyme this tretye shal suffise

Dispose you / to kepe it in your mynde

The doctrine whiche for you I deuyse            514

And doubteth not / ful wel ye shal it finde

To your honour / enrolle it vp and bynde

Right in your breste / and at your riper age

I shal wryte to you / herof the surplusage       518

This is enough
for the present.
Mind you attend
to it,

and when you're
older I'll write
you the rest.

---

Plesaunt wordis I avyse you to them saye,

  & in all wyse do ye your delygence

511    To do them plesyre and reverence.

[Hill's Text.]

¶ And at this tyme this treatise shall suffice ;

  Do pose you to kepe it in your mynde,

  the doctryne which for you I devyse ;

  & dowteth not, full well ye shall yt fynde

516    To your honowre ; enrolle yt vp & bynde

  Right in your brest, & at your ryper age

  I shall write you here-of the surplusage.

[75]

Goo, litle childe, and who doth you Appose,
Seying, youre quaire kepeth non accordaunce,
Tell [hym], as yite neyther of ryme ne prose     521
    Ye be experte ; pray hym of sufferaunce ;
    Childer must be of childly gouernaunce,
      And they must also entredet [1] be       [1] *Read entreted.*
      Wyth esy thyng, [and not] of subtilte.     525

[76]

Youre lytil quaier summitteth euery where
To coreccion and beneuolence,
But where enuie is, loke hit come not there,     528
    For eny thing kepith youre trety thense ;
    Enuie is full of frowarde reprehense,
      And howe to hurte liethe euere in awayte,
      Kepeth youre quaiere, that hit be not her baite.

**EXPLICIT.**

**DOMINE, SALUUM FAC REGEM.**

---

¶ Go, litill Iohñ, & who doth you oppose,     *[Hill's Text.]*
520    sayenge your quayre, kepeth non accordavnce ;
    Tell hym as ȝet neythere in ryme ne prose
    ye ben experte ; pray hym of suffraunce.
    Chyldren [1] muste be of childy gouernavnce,     [1] *MS. Clyldren.*
524    & also thei muste entreted be
    With easy thynge, & not with subtilte.

[75]

Go lytyl Iohn / and who doth you appose
Sayng your quayer / kepe non accordance
Telle hym as yet / neyther in ryme ne prose
Ye ben expert / praye hym of suffrance
Chyldren muste be / of chyldly gouernañce
And also they muste entretyde be
With esy thing / and not with subtylte

521

525

Whoever
questions you,

say you are not
yet up in rime or
prose.

[76]

Go lytil quayer / submytte you euery where
Vnder correction of benyuolence
And where enuye is / loke ye come not there
For ony thinge / kepe your tretye thens
Enuye is ful of froward reprehens
And how to hurte / lyeth euer in a wayte
Kepe your quayer / that it be not ther bayte

528

532

Little book,
I submit you to
correction :

but go not where
envy is.

Explicit the book of curtesye.

¶ Go, lytill quayer, submyte you euery where
vnder correccion of benevolence ;
& wher envy ys, loke you cum not there,
ffor any thyng kepe your treatye thens;
Envye ys full of froward reprehens,
& how to hurte lyeth ever in a-wayte ;
kepe your quayre that yt be not ther bayte.

528

532

[Hill's Text.]

Here endyth A lytyll treatyse
called the boke of curtesy or litill Iohan.

# INDEX.